Happy Valen

Olivia and T━━━

love,
Gram

Rol CWade

The Adventures of Gwen Penguin
Copyright © 2021 Robin Wade

ISBN: 978-1-63381-245-1

Designed and produced by:
Maine Authors Publishing
12 High Street, Thomaston, Maine
www.maineauthorspublishing.com

Printed in the United States of America

THE ADVENTURES OF
GWEN PENGUIN

BY ROBIN WADE

Majestic icebergs drifted on a sea of blue and green.
Gwen Penguin asked her parents,
"Where do the icebergs go, when they can't be seen?"

Gwen's family always lived near islands of ice and snow.
"They come and go with the tides," her parents explained.
"We really just don't know."

Constantly curious, Gwen's decision was quite swift.
"Dear parents, I need to know where the icebergs go,
so I'll follow them as they drift."

Gwen's mother watched her daughter leave,
and then she shed a tear.
Gwen's ice raft grew smaller on the horizon,
and soon it disappeared.

The sun warmed Gwen's face as the ice raft cooled her feet.
Beneath her was a mighty ocean, the water dark and deep.

A little green crab surfaced as Gwen drifted under the moonlit sky.
"You've been drifting quite a while, Penguin, and I am curious to know why."
"I am following the icebergs. Do you know where they go?"

Crab thought for a moment and then replied with a gentle "No."
"Please join me, Crab," said Gwen. "Come as an ocean guide
and a friendly companion to travel by my side."

Three tiny pink birds flew down to the sea.
"Where are you going?" asked the little birds three.
"We are following the icebergs. Do you know where they go?"
The birds chirped in harmony, "No, no, no."

"Please join us!" said Gwen. "And from your bird's-eye view,
watch over us as we drift upon the vast ocean blue."

A young, gentle whale surfaced beside the herd.
"Where are you going, Penguin, Crab, and three Birds?"
The friends responded, "We are following the icebergs."

Gwen asked the Whale, "Do you know where the icebergs go?"
The Whale thought for a moment and then spouted, "No."

Whale was quite happy to join in their quest,
and they all slowly drifted north by northwest.

The seas were calm, and as the birds sang a song,
they noticed something else in the water was drifting along.

"Look!" said Gwen, "Underneath the surface, within the deep beautiful sea, there's collection of nets, and straws, and plastic debris!"

Suddenly the wind blew harder, and the waves became so rough
that avoiding the nets and floating debris proved to be awfully tough.

As Gwen and her friends were surfing atop a giant wave,
they came upon a helpless turtle hoping to be saved.

Turtle was entangled in a red net that held him tight.
When Turtle spotted Gwen and her friends, he knew rescue was in sight.

Gwen said, "Let's work as a team to free Turtle's neck and flippers!"
Gwen, Whale, and the three Birds tugged at the net.
"Crab, use your strong claws as clippers!"

"What is this horrible stuff?" Gwen asked Turtle, who now was free.
Turtle sighed, "It's pollution from the humans
who throw their trash in the rivers, lakes, and seas."

Gwen and her friends banded together to gather the flotsam and debris.
They towed the bundle to a passing boat that sailed upon the sea.

The people on the boat were glad to take the nets and pollution,
telling Gwen and all her friends, "We, too, are seeking a solution."

Gwen and her friends sang a song as they drifted along with glee:
"Take care of nets and plastic for every creature
who lives on the land, in the air, or the sea."

As sunset colors reflected on calm and glassy water,
Gwen and friends met two penguins—Glen and his little daughter.

"Do you know where the icebergs go?" asked Gwen to Glen and Jen.
They said, "We don't know where they go,"
so they joined the band of friends.

Both Gwen and Glen were adventurous and wise.
They shared feelings of respect as they gazed into each other's eyes.

The waters warmed as they drifted north.
The icebergs melted into the sea.
"I guess it's time to go home," said Gwen.
"Who wants to go back with me?"

They all returned home with Gwen.
The winds and currents were swift.
Gwen, with her new family and friends,
would no longer be adrift.

Gwen's family was overjoyed to see their daughter had returned.
"Our dearest Gwen, gone so long, please tell us what you have learned."

"Beyond the horizon, the icebergs drift at will.
Wind and currents move them; they're never completely still.
As we followed the icebergs north, warm waters melted their massive size.
They disappeared beneath the surface before our very eyes.
We learned there is a problem with fishing nets and pollution.
But while some humans pollute, others work toward a solution."

"Family and friends, on the next adventure, come along with me.
We'll drift with the blue and white icebergs and sing in sweet harmony:
'Let's take care of nets and plastic for all the creatures,
who live on the land, in the air, or the sea.'"